Juanito Counts to Ten
Johnny cuenta hasta diez

a Bilingual Counting Book

written by **Lee Merrill Byrd**

illustrations by **Francisco Delgado**

oh, Juanito!
He's always counting out kisses. Look!

¡Ay Johnny!
Siempre va contando besos. ¡Mira!

ONE little tiny one
for his big sister,
who thinks she's the boss.

UNO chiquitito para
su hermana, que piensa
que es la mera mera.

TWO big ones
for his daddy, the
pitcher whose arm
never quits.

DOS

grandotes para su papá, el pitcher
que nunca se cansa.

TRES bien cariñosos

para su mamá,
que descansa en el sofá.

FOUR served up with hugs
for Mari, his teacher.

CUATRO besos con abrazos
para Mari, su maestra.

FIVE
he sends
to Birdie in
the mail.

CINCO
se los manda
a Birdie
por correo.

SIX he blows to Patty
who cuts his hair.

SEIS los tira al viento para Patty
que le corta el cabello.

SEVEN

he dreams
of for Beatriz,
the girl who won't
kiss him back.

SIETE

sueña con
darle a Beatriz,
la niña que no le
regresa los besos.

EIGHT he plants on Stray Gray.

OCHO bien plantados para El Gato Gris.

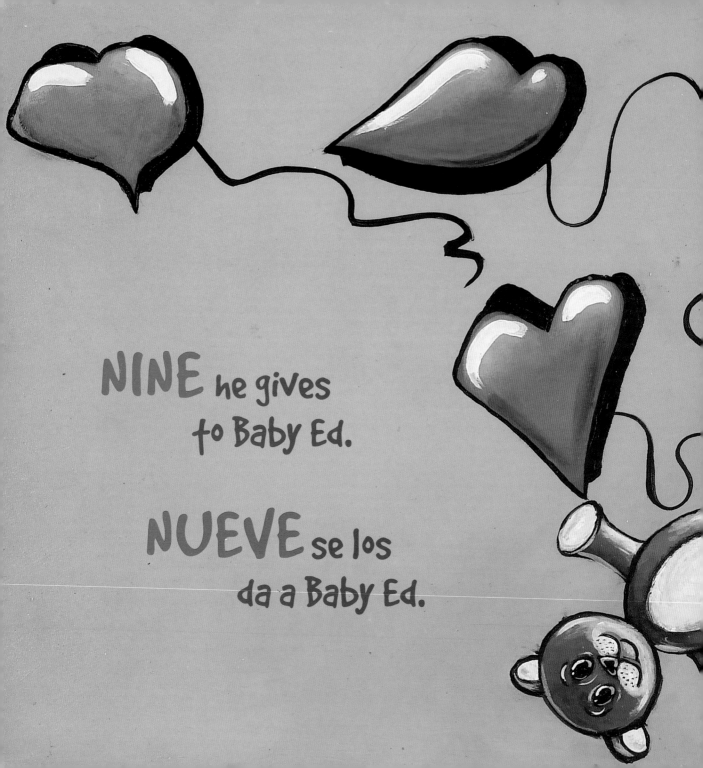

NINE he gives
to Baby Ed.

NUEVE se los
da a Baby Ed.

NEVER!

¡NUNCA!

Siempre va contando
besos y ¡a mí me
tocan DIEZ !

FIRST EDITION
10 9 8 7 6 5 4 3 2 1

LIBRARY OF CONGRESS CATALOGING-IN-PUBLICATION DATA

Byrd, Lee Merrill.
  Juanito Counts to Ten = Johnny cuenta hasta diez / by Lee Merrill Byrd ; illustrated by Francisco Delgado.— 1st ed.
    p. cm.
  Summary: Four-year-old Johnny loves to count out kisses, and he counts them in both English and Spanish.
  ISBN 978-1-933693-12-5
  [1. Kissing—Fiction. 2. Spanish language materials—Bilingual. 3. Counting.] I. Title: Johnny cuenta hasta diez.
II. Delgado, Francisco, 1974- ill. III. Title.
  PZ73.B95 2005
  [E]--dc22
                              2005013982

For Johnny Andrew and Pedro, Hannah, Silly Lolly, Baby Ed, Birdie and Santiago.

Juanito Counts to Ten / Johnny cuenta hasta diez was inspired by two boys, Pedro and Johnny, and is dedicated to all the young children in the world. May they never cease to overflow with kisses!

PEDRO & JOHNNY   *photograph by Francis Delgado*

Translation by David Dorado Romo, edited by Luis Humberto Crosthwaite.

Thanks to Sharon Franco for her eye on the text, as always.

Book and cover design by JB Bryan of La Alameda Press.